W9-BEU-552

For Anna and Maya. ~ Aimee Aryal

For Dave Vinson. ~ Brad V

www.mascotbooks.com

Hello, Paws!

©2008 Mascot Books. All Rights Reserved. No part of this publication may
be reproduced, stored in a retrieval system or transmitted in any form
by any means electronic, mechanical, or photocopying, recording or
otherwise without the permission of the author.

For more information, please contact:
Mascot Books
560 Herndon Parkway #120
Herndon, VA 20170
info@mascotbooks.com

CPSIA Code: PRT0214B
ISBN-10: 1932888748
ISBN-13: 9781932888744

Major League Baseball trademarks and copyrights are used with
permission of Major League Baseball Properties, Inc.

Printed in the United States

Hello, Paws!™

Aimee Aryal

Illustrated by Brad Vinson

MASCOT BOOKS

It was a beautiful day in Detroit, Michigan.
Paws, the Tigers mascot, was on his way to
the ballpark for a baseball game.

As Paws walked through Greektown,
Tigers fans cheered, "Hello, Paws!"

Paws walked down Woodward Avenue
on the way to the game.

In front of the ballpark, Paws ran into lots of Tigers fans. They cheered, "Hello, Paws!"

Paws arrived on the field just in time
for batting practice. Each player took
swings to get ready for the game.

As the team's best hitter stepped
to home plate, he said, "Hello, Paws!"

After batting practice, the grounds crew
proudly prepared the field for play.

As the grounds crew worked,
they hollered, "Hello, Paws!"

Paws was feeling hungry. He grabbed a few snacks and a Tigers pennant at the concession stand.

As he made his way back to the field,
a family shouted, "Hello, Paws!"

Each Tigers player stood on the third baseline as the home team was introduced.

Paws received the largest applause!
Fans roared, "Hello, Paws!"

"PLAY BALL!" yelled the umpire. The Tigers pitcher delivered a fastball to start the game. "STRIKE ONE!" called the umpire.

The umpire noticed Paws nearby
and said, "Hello, Paws!"

Paws went into the bleachers to visit his
fans. Everyone was excited to see Paws.

A family waved and called out,
"Hello, Paws!"

It was now time for the seventh inning stretch. Paws led the crowd as everyone sang "Take Me Out To The Ballgame™!"

Young Tigers fans danced on the dugout with Paws. They cheered, "Hello, Paws!"

In the bottom of the ninth inning, a Tigers player hit a game-winning home run over the right field fence.

The team gathered at home
plate to celebrate the victory. The
players chanted, "Tigers win,
Paws! Tigers win!"

After the game, Paws was tired. It had been
a long day at the ballpark. Paws walked home
and went straight to bed.

Goodnight, Paws!

Have a book idea?

Contact us at:

Mascot Books

560 Herndon Parkway

Suite 120

Herndon, VA

info@mascotbooks.com | www.mascotbooks.com